This book belongs to

_____

_____

_____

My room and me

My little bookrack

My sister

My mom

My dad

My friends

My grandpa

My grandma

My best friend

My uncle

My aunt

My cousin

My pet

My school

My karate class

My favourite theme park

My favourite teacher

My favourite colour—blue

My favourite ice cream

My birthday

Visit to a circus

Movie hall

Zoo

Amusement park

Holidaying in a national park

My favourite game, basketball

Treehouse in my garden

Tent in my garden

Favourite holiday destination

My bicycle

My favourite festival, Halloween